Tiny Tiger

Barbara deRubertis
Illustrated by Eva Vagreti Cockrille

The Kane Press
New York

Cover Design: Sheryl Kagen

Library of Congress Cataloging-in-Publication Data

DeRubertis, Barbara.
Tiny Tiger/Barbara deRubertis; illustrated by Eva Vagreti Cockrille.
p.   cm.
"A Let's read together book."

Summary: Tiny Tiger is too shy to play with the other cats., but then old Riley Lion
gives him some wise advice.
ISBN 1-57565-024-X (pbk. : alk. paper)
[1. Bashfulness--Fiction. 2. Tigers--Fiction. 3. Stories in rhyme.]
I. Vagreti Cockrille, Eva, ill. II. Title.
PZ8.3.D455Ti 1997   96-53272
[E]--dc21   CIP
                                                      AC

10 9 8 7 6 5

First published in the United States of America in 1997 by The Kane Press.
Printed in China.

LET'S READ TOGETHER is a registered trademark of The Kane Press.

Tiny Tiger
is so shy.
He wishes he had
friends. Oh, my!

The other kids
just pass him by.

They do not see
poor Tiny cry.

He sees the others
ride on bikes.

He sees the others
hike on hikes.

He sees the others
slide on slides.
Tiny sees them
while he hides.

Riley Lion
blinks his eyes.
He thinks he knows
why Tiny cries.

Riley's kind
and very wise.
If he can help
a friend, he tries.

"Hi there, Tiny!"
  Riley smiles.
"I've been watching
  you awhile.

"I've seen you hide.
  I've seen you cry.
  I've seen that you
  are very shy.

"I was once
  as shy as you.
  I'll help you if you
  want me to.

"But first, I'd like
for you to try
a slice of Simon's
ice cream pie!"

A slice of pie?
At Simon's shop?
Tiny gives
a happy hop.

Simon asks,
"What kind of pie?"

"The ice cream pie!"
is their reply.

The pie arrives.
It's pink and white.
With great delight
they take a bite.

16

They talk and talk.
They eat their pie.
With Riley, Tiny
is not shy.

Riley smiles.
His smile is wide.
And Tiny feels
the smile inside.

Tiny says,
"You are so nice!
Can you help me
with some advice?"

Riley says,
"I *can* help you!
  There are two things
  that you can do.

"When kids you know
  come talk to you,
  talk back to them!
  And smile, too!"

Tiny Tiger
says, "I'll try!
I'll talk and smile!
I won't be shy!

"Thank you, Riley!"
Tiny cries.
Then Tiny gives
his friend "high fives!"

"Good-bye!" he calls.
He flies outside.
And Riley's eyes
are filled with pride.

Tiny thinks.
"Now I must try
my friend's advice.
I *won't* be shy."

Mike the Panther
says, "Hi, Tiny!"
Tiny smiles.
His smile is shiny!

Tiny then replies, "Hi, Mike! Would you like to try my bike?"

Tiny Tiger
smiles with pride
as he and Mike
ride side by side!